# GEORGE AND MARTHA RISE AND SHINE

# For My Father

The stories in this book were originally published by Houghton Mifflin Company in *George and Martha: Rise and Shine,* 1976. All rights reserved.
For information about permission to reproduce selections from this book, write to Permissions, Houghton Mifflin Harcourt Publishing Company, 215 Park Avenue South, New York, New York 10003.

www.hmhbooks.com

First Green Light Readers edition 2011

SANDPIPER and the SANDPIPER logo are trademarks of Houghton Mifflin Harcourt Publishing Company.

Green Light Readers and its logo are trademarks of Houghton Mifflin Harcourt Publishing Company, registered in the United States of America and/or other jurisdictions.

The Library of Congress Cataloging-in-Publication Data is on file.

ISBN 978-0-547-14425-2 hardcover
ISBN 978-0-547-57687-9 paperback

Manufactured in Singapore
TWP 10 9 8 7 6 5 4 3 2 1

4500287688

Ages: 7–8
Grade: 2
Guided Reading Level: L
Reading Recovery Level: 19

# GEORGE AND MARTHA RISE AND SHINE

*written and illustrated by*

JAMES MARSHALL

sandpiper

Green Light Readers

HOUGHTON MIFFLIN HARCOURT

BOSTON   NEW YORK

# THREE STORIES ABOUT TWO FINE FRIENDS

# STORY NUMBER ONE

# THE FIBBER

One day George wanted to impress Martha.

"I used to be a champion jumper," he said.

Martha raised an eyebrow.

"And," said George, "I used to be a wicked pirate."

"Hmmm," said Martha.

George tried harder. "Once I was even a famous snake charmer!"

"Oh, goody," said Martha.

7

Martha went to the closet and got out Sam.

"Here's a snake for you to charm."

"Eeeek," cried George.

And he jumped right out of his chair.

"It's only a toy *stuffed* snake," said Martha. "I'm surprised a famous snake charmer is such a scaredy-cat."

"I told some fibs," said George.

"For shame," said Martha.

"But you can see what a good jumper I am," said George.

"That's true," said Martha.

11

# STORY NUMBER
## Two

# THE EXPERIMENT

Martha was in her laboratory.

"What are you doing?" asked George.

"I'm studying fleas," said Martha.

"Cute little critters," said George.

"You don't understand," said Martha.

"This is serious. This is science."

The next day, George noticed that Martha was scratching a lot. She looked uncomfortable.

George bought Martha some special soap.

After her shower Martha felt much better.

"I think I'll stop studying fleas," said Martha.

"Good idea," said George.

"I think I'll study bees instead," said Martha.

"Oh dear," said George.

# STORY NUMBER 3

# THE PICNIC

One Saturday morning, George wanted
to sleep late.
"I love sleeping late," said George.
But Martha had other ideas.
She wanted to go on a picnic.
"Here she comes!" said George to himself.

Martha did her best to get George out of bed.

"Picnic time!" sang Martha.

But George didn't budge.

Martha played a tune on her saxophone.

George put little balls of cotton in his ears
and pulled up the covers.

Martha tickled George's toes.

"Stop it!" said George.

"Picnic time!" sang Martha.

"But I'm *not* going on a picnic!" said George.

"Oh yes you *are!*" said his friend.

Martha had a clever idea.

"This is such hard work," she said, huffing and puffing.

"But I'm not going to help," said George.

"I'm getting tired," said Martha.

George had fun on the picnic.

"I'm so glad we came," said George.

But Martha wasn't listening.

She had fallen asleep.

Search for these words from *George and Martha: Rise and Shine*:

fib, glad, surprise, budge, critter, laboratory, picnic

| Q | E | F | D | V | H | C | J | N | D | S | L |
|---|---|---|---|---|---|---|---|---|---|---|---|
| T | G | L | A | B | O | R | A | T | O | R | Y |
| P | S | U | R | P | R | I | S | E | D | U | R |
| G | I | A | Z | F | P | T | E | C | M | A | F |
| L | B | C | L | U | N | T | G | G | S | L | F |
| A | R | M | N | J | B | E | B | Z | D | H | K |
| D | S | E | I | I | E | R | I | C | I | U | L |
| Q | Y | T | N | X | C | V | F | J | F | A | B |

Choose one of these words from *George and Martha: Rise and Shine*:

budge, tickles, laboratory, impress, uncomfortable, notices

1. George fibs because he wants to

   _____Martha.

2. Martha feels very_____when

   fleas start biting her.

3. George_____Martha scratching

   at fleas and gives her special soap.

4. To try to get George out of bed, Martha

   _____his toes.

5. Martha studies fleas in her_____.

6. George is not a morning person. Martha can't

   even make him_____!

1. impress 2. uncomfortable 3. notices 4. tickles 5. laboratory 6. budge

Match the questions on the top with their correct answers below!

1. George tells Martha he is good at what two things?

2. What is Martha studying in her laboratory?

3. Why does Martha want George to get out of bed?

4. What does Martha get from the closet?

5. What does Martha do to wake George up?

6. How does George help Martha?

7. Why does George jump out of his chair?

Brings her special soap to wash away the fleas

Plays the saxophone and tickles his toes

He thinks the toy snake is real

Fleas

To go on a picnic

A toy stuffed snake

Jumping and charming snakes

# Fun activities for home!

1. Make a list of all of the things you would take on a picnic.

2. Draw a picture of your favorite critter.

3. Try to remember any fibs you might have told recently.

# More Reading Practice!

Cut out flash cards on the following pages. Then practice reading the words. Sentence clues are on the back, so Mom or Dad can help and practice with you.

| Good | Once |
|------|------|
| her | an |
| best | toy |

"_____I was even a famous snake charmer!"

"I think I'll stop studying fleas," said Martha. "_____idea," said George.

Martha raised_____eyebrow.

After_____shower Martha felt much better.

"It's only a_____*stuffed* snake, said Martha.

Martha did her_____to get George out of bed.